D0589625

With special thanks to Conrad Mason

Dedicated to Arthur Mason

ORCHARD BOOKS

First published in Great Britain in 2023 by Hodder & Stoughton

3 5 7 9 10 8 6 4 2

Text © Beast Quest Limited 2023
Cover and inside illustrations by Juan Calle
© Beast Quest Limited 2023
Illustration: Juan Calle (Liberum Donum). Cover colour: Santiago Calle.
Shading: Juan Calle and Luis Suarez

Series created by Beast Quest Limited, London

A CIP catalogue record for this book is available from the British Library.

ISBN 978 1 40836 803 9

Printed in Great Britain

The paper and board used in this book are made from wood from responsible sources.

Orchard Books
An imprint of Hachette Children's Group
Part of Hodder & Stoughton
Carmelite House, 50 Victoria Embankment, London EC4Y 0DZ

An Hachette UK Company
www.hachette.co.uk
www.hachettechildrens.co.uk

SPACE WARS

DROID DOG STRIKE

ADAM BLADE

ORCHARD

Avantia ...

Once upon a time, it was a lush, green planet with sparkling blue oceans. A haven for life in all its forms, and a home to eight billion people. A place of incredible technology and culture.

Until the Void ...

In Avantia City, it struck on a clear day at the height of summer. No one saw it coming. No one understood it. And no one was prepared.

First there was a roar, like distant thunder. Then a swirling vortex ripped apart the sky, streaked with vivid green and purple storms of electricity. It was vast, like the mouth of a monster.

As earthquakes shook the ground, the citizens scrambled into any craft that could fly. They fled their homes, their very atmosphere ... and from the darkness of space, they watched the Void swallow their planet, leaving nothing behind.

For most, it was the end.

But for those lucky few, the survivors ...

It was only the beginning.

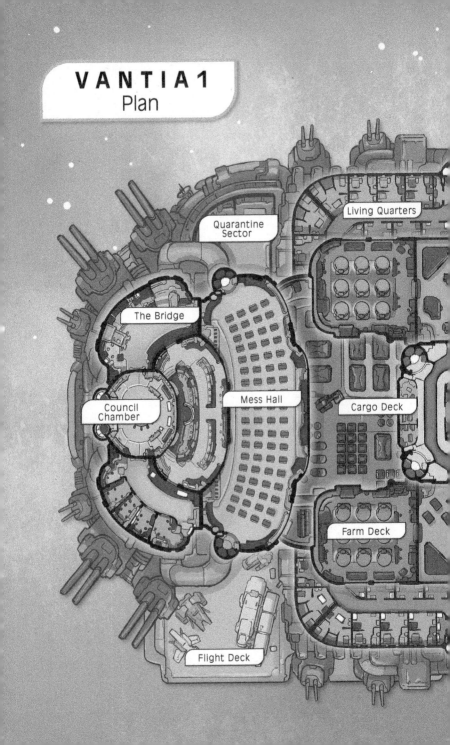

VANTIA 1
Plan

Quarantine Sector

Living Quarters

The Bridge

Council Chamber

Mess Hall

Cargo Deck

Farm Deck

Flight Deck

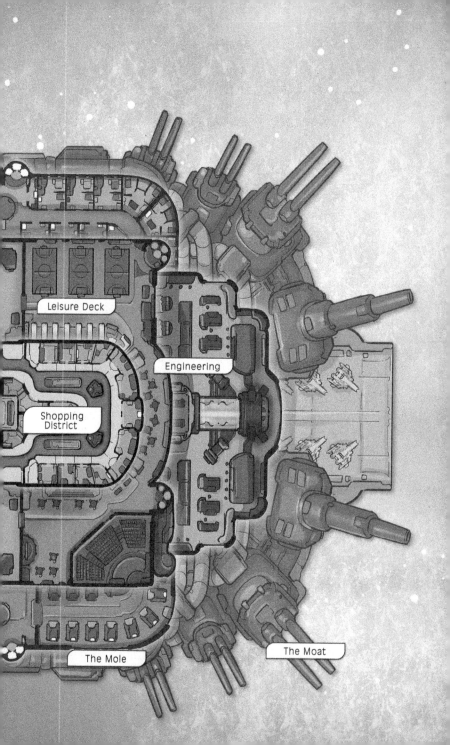

Leisure Deck

Engineering

Shopping
District

The Mole

The Moat

1: Harry Hugo is a talented apprentice engineer, and there's nothing he can't fix.

2: Ava Achebe is a cadet, training to be one of Vantia1's elite space pilots.

3: Zo Harkman, Chief Engineer, has taken care of Harry ever since his parents disappeared.

4: Markus Knox, another cadet, *thinks* he's brave and daring ...

5: Governor Knox is in charge of running Vantia1 and protecting all the station's inhabitants.

6: Admiral Achebe is the commander of the space fleet, and gives orders to the pilots.

CONTENTS

CHAPTER 1

GHOST STATION

*"**Are you done** yet?"* asked Ava, for the third time. She was drumming her fingers impatiently on the dining table.

"I ..." muttered Harry, "am ..." – he slotted the upper arm unit into his shoulder socket – "... done!"

With a *hiss* of hydraulics and a

satisfying *clunk*, the robotic arm locked into place, and a green light glowed on the back of the hand.

A smile spread across Harry's face. He had lost the last version of his robotic arm in a fight with a giant robotic spider, and it was a relief to feel whole again. "Check it out! It's online."

"Nice!" Ava leaned across the table to admire Harry's new creation. "What does that bumpy bit do?"

Using his free hand, Harry clicked open the housing on his robotic index finger. "Laser cutter," he said proudly, showing Ava the unit. "It's not easy making one so small."

Ava rolled her eyes. "We get it,

you're an engineering genius."

Harry grinned back at her. "Well, if you think that's impressive, wait till you see the extendable  high-tensile grappling hook."

"Hmm." Ava raised an eyebrow. "Anyone would think you're planning on having some kind of adventure or something."

Harry tried to smile, but this time he couldn't manage it. There was only one adventure on his mind. *Rescuing my parents.* He couldn't stop picturing their faces, pale and scared, on the holographic transmission Vellis had shown him. The evil scientist was holding Harry's parents captive on the Avantian moon of Gwildor, forcing them to work on something he called his "project".

Meanwhile Harry and Ava were stuck on Vantia1, hanging out in Zo Harkman's quarters all day long.

"Have you spoken to your mum yet?" asked Harry. Ava's mother was Admiral Achebe, the military commander on Vantia1. If anyone could convince

Governor Knox to authorise a rescue, it was her.

Ava's face fell. "I'm sorry, Harry. I tried, but she just told me to be patient. They won't send a mission until they've gathered more intelligence."

"Being patient won't stop Vellis," said Harry.

"Hey, I'm on your side," said Ava, throwing up her hands. "I'm sick of this too. And the station's so … *empty* now, with everyone shipped off to Vantia2." She gave him a sly grin. "You know, I'm even starting to miss Markus Knox."

Harry let out a snort of laughter. Markus was the Governor's son, but unlike her, he was an arrogant bully. *At least he's one thing I don't have to worry about right now.*

Harry pushed the thought of his parents from his mind and flexed his robotic fingers. They whirred faintly, but the movement was smooth – just as responsive as the fingers on his real hand. "Hey, toss me an apple," he said.

Ava took one from the fruit bowl. "Catch!"

Harry reached and caught it with the robotic hand. "Looks like the spatial programming is on point." He lifted the apple to take a bite.

Ka-chunk!

The robotic fingers closed suddenly, crushing the apple. Chunks of fruit went flying, spattering Harry's face with juice. He blinked and wiped himself down with a sleeve.

"I take back the *engineering genius* part," said Ava.

Harry frowned. "It's just a minor setback. I'll run a diagnostic on the grip. Hey, you want to come? The tool's down in Zo's lab."

Ava yawned. "Sure. Beats sitting around all day waiting for something to happen."

✪

A few minutes later, the Mole doors swished open on the Engineering Deck.

Harry and Ava stepped out into a corridor that was just as deserted as the rest of Vantia1. *It's like a ghost station,* thought Harry, with a shiver. Apart from Harry and Ava, only a few essential personnel had stayed behind while Vantia1 was repaired after Vellis's last attack.

The laboratory was at the end of the corridor. Harry scanned his ID card and the door slid smoothly open. But as they stepped into the large, gleaming white space, he was surprised to see that they were not alone.

"Hello, you two," said Harkman, giving them a nod from the far side of the lab. Harry's guardian was a large man with neatly combed grey hair and bright blue eyes. Standing with him were Admiral Achebe, shaven-headed and straight-backed in her uniform, and Governor Knox herself in her purple robes of office. *The three most important people in the whole station!*

Only Harkman had turned to greet them. The others were staring intently at an image floating above a blue-lit projection table. It looked like a three-dimensional

spider's web, with a hundred glowing, coloured nodes.

"Intruder alert," said a robotic voice, and a sleek white security droid hovered across the room. "Please leave immediately."

"Belay that," said Harkman, waving a hand impatiently. "Access granted."

The droid slid to a halt and powered down.

"What's going on?" asked Ava, eyes wide.

Admiral Achebe turned at her daughter's voice and beckoned them over. Harry and Ava went to join the adults, their faces all glowing blue in the light of the projection table.

"It's some kind of molecular model, right?" said Harry, peering at the rotating image.

"Indeed," said Harkman. "We sent a recon drone to your parents' old laboratory on Avantia. We were hoping it would turn up some evidence about how the Void was created."

"And did it?" asked Ava.

Harkman nodded. "Most of the lab files were scrambled, of course. But there were a few encrypted logs in Vellis's name. That's where we found this."

Harry tensed. Vellis had worked with his parents, long ago, before he had turned against them all.

"Go on then," said Ava. "What is it?"

"It's Tallium."

Harry looked up at the new voice. It was A.D.U.R.O., the station's AI, whose face had materialised on the far side of the projection table. Her smooth features were as expressionless as ever beneath her shock of spiky white hair.

"Tallium is a highly unstable radioactive element, capable of releasing vast amounts of energy," explained A.D.U.R.O.

"It looks like Vellis was experimenting with it," said Admiral Achebe. "And those experiments went badly wrong. We think they caused a meltdown that generated the Void."

"I've heard of Tallium before," said Harry. "It's rare, isn't it?"

Harkman and the other grown-ups shared a glance.

"There's something you're not telling me," said Harry.

Governor Knox gave a nod, and Harkman sighed. "The only place we've ever found Tallium is on Gwildor."

A sick feeling came over Harry. "He must be extracting it!" He pointed at the projection. "That's why he needs my parents."

Harkman shifted uncomfortably. "Even if Vellis has a base on Avantia's moon, we don't know that he's using Tallium."

Harry's heart was racing. "But if he is? Whatever Vellis is working on, it's bound to be something dangerous. Maybe even more dangerous than the Void. This isn't just about Mum and Dad. It's about Vantia1. It's about the whole *galaxy*!"

He turned to Governor Knox. She was still staring at the spinning model of the Tallium molecule, apparently lost in thought. "Please…" he begged. "We've got to send a rescue mission."

"Harry," said Harkman, gently. "We've already discussed this. It's not for you to—"

"No."

Everyone stared at the Governor. It was the first word she had spoken. But now she looked up at them, her hawk-like eyes glinting with purpose.

"Cadet Hugo is right. Now we know

what Vellis is capable of, we have a duty to do something. Ready a ship, Admiral Achebe. Gather a team. We're going to Gwildor!"

CHAPTER 2

RESCUE MISSION

"You're not seriously bringing that thing?" said Ava.

"You bet I am," said Harry, patting the soft saddle of his gleaming red Space Stallion. "You know how many jams he's got me out of? We're partners."

"Darn tootin'," said the Space Stallion,

in its smooth robotic voice. Harry had programmed it to speak just like the cowboys in the ancient films that Zo Harkman liked to watch.

The Stallion was propped up out of the way in a corner of the Flight Deck. The hangar bustled with activity as the few engineers left on Vantia1 readied a ship to cross into the Void. It was a mid-sized vessel, Tagus Class, big enough to carry a maximum crew of thirty.

And I'm going to be one of that crew.

A shiver of anticipation ran through Harry at the thought. *Hold on, Mum and Dad. I'm coming for you.*

"You are seriously not bringing that thing," came a stern voice from behind. Harry turned to see Zo Harkman glowering at him.

"My thoughts exactly," said Ava, crossing her arms.

"But—"

"For the tenth time, this is just reconnaissance, Harry," interrupted Zo. "It's not a rescue mission. We're going to get as close to Gwildor as we can, then run some basic scans. That's *it*."

"Oh yeah?" said Harry. "If it's just recon, why are *they* coming?" He pointed across the flight deck to a troop of twelve marines dressed in black body armour and drawn up in two ranks. Captain Tex, a big, bearded man with a constellation of stars tattooed on his neck, was checking their phase rifles.

Harkman rolled his eyes. "It's a *precaution*, Harry. Governor Knox isn't taking any chances, and you're not either. Understood?"

"I guess," muttered Harry.

"If you ask me, you should be grateful the Admiral is letting you come at all," said Harkman. "And bringing that hobby-horse of yours? Out of the question."

The Space Stallion let out an indignant bleep. "Pardon me, mister, but I ain't seen too many hobby-horses got a Class 4 phase-rocket launcher and twin Magror sponson blasters."

"Not helping, buddy," groaned Harry.

"The Stallion stays behind," said

Harkman, firmly. "I mean it, Harry."

"Well, that's that," said Ava, as Harkman strode off to help the crew.

"Is it, though?"

Ava raised an eyebrow. "I know that look, Harry. Something tells me you're about to do something foolish."

"Foolish, or brilliant?" Harry turned around. "Make yourself scarce, partner."

"You got it," said the Stallion. A soft hum filled the air, then – *fzoosh!* – the Stallion vanished into thin air.

"Whoa!" Ava reached out cautiously. "Is it still there?"

Harry took hold of the invisible handlebars. "Not bad, huh? It's a cloaking mechanism."

"OK," agreed Ava. "This time, I'll admit I'm impressed."

"Now help me get the Stallion into the hold," said Harry, flicking the kickstand up with his toe. "Before anyone figures out what we're doing."

"I guess what Harkman doesn't know won't hurt him," said Ava. "Come on then. Let's get this hobby-horse stowed."

A swirl of lights, a thundering in his ears and then ...

Silence.

Darkness filled the viewing screen. A darkness pinpricked by stars. Harry sagged against the safety harness. *Made it.*

"What on ..." gasped Harkman. "What *was* that?"

"*That* was crossing into the Void," said Ava.

"You get used to it," added Harry. "Kind of." His own stomach was still churning, his vision dancing. He blinked and fought down the urge to be sick.

Zo was sitting up ahead in the cockpit

of the Tagus, along with Admiral Achebe, the pilot and the navigator. Harry and Ava sat behind with the marines, all strapped into crash seats. The soldiers were shifting uneasily, checking they were all in one piece and groggily shaking their heads.

"Your shell protection technology seems highly effective," said Admiral Achebe. "Good work, Harkman."

Harry's guardian looked a little green. "Personally, I think it needs adjusting."

Harry grinned at Ava.

"Admiral," said the navigator. "I've located Gwildor. It's no longer orbiting Avantia."

"The Void must have disrupted the

gravitational field," said Harry.

"Indeed." Achebe nodded. "Set a course. Once we've carried out our scans, we'll report back to the Governor on Vantia1."

"Aye aye, Admiral."

Harry felt the vessel tilt as the pilot fired up the engines and steered them through the blackness of space.

All around, the marines got up to stretch their legs in the artificial gravity. They chatted in low voices, chuckling about old comrades, space stations they had visited and pirates they had taken into custody. Even Ava was listening, snorting with laughter at a story about an uptight lieutenant.

Harry wished he could relax. His eyes darted to the corner of the ship where they had hidden the cloaked Stallion. Somehow, he had a feeling that he and the bike hadn't ridden their last rodeo.

"Visual on screen," said the navigator.

Craning his neck, Harry saw a moon coming into view up ahead. It was a swirling reddish-brown sphere, surrounded by rings of space dust.

"Gwildor," breathed Ava, eyes wide. "It's beautiful."

Harry nodded grimly. All he could think of was his mum and dad, held captive somewhere on the surface.

"Initiate scan," ordered the Admiral.

Harkman tapped at the control panel,

then frowned. "Negative. There's some sort of signal blocker."

"I guess Vellis saw us coming," muttered Harry. "What now?"

"I'm working on it," said Harkman. "If we can just override the—"

"Look!" Ava clapped a hand on Harry's shoulder, making him jump. She was pointing through the viewscreen.

Peering closer, Harry saw it – a speck, hurting towards them from Gwildor, getting bigger by the second. His heart rate sped up. "What is that?"

"Looks like a vessel," said the pilot, checking the scan. "It's small. A transport pod, most likely. No weapons on board."

"But it's heading straight for us," said

Achebe, frowning. "Captain Tex?"

The leader of the marines was already at the gunnery station, adjusting the targeting visor and bringing the blasters online. "Got a lock," he grunted. The big man never spoke more than he had to.

"Open a comms channel," ordered Achebe. "Attention, unknown vessel! Do not approach. Repeat, do not approach."

"It's holding course," said the pilot.

Harry held his breath. The ship was close enough to be seen clearly now – a battered old escape pod several generations out of date. There couldn't be room on board for more than a handful of people.

His skin prickled with a strange sense of anticipation.

"Fire a warning shot," said Achebe.

A glowing green tracer arced across the viewing screen like a firework. But still the pod came hurtling towards them, not even slowing.

"No good, Admiral," rumbled Tex.

"Say the word and I'll blow it to bits."

Admiral Achebe frowned, calculating.

"Remember what the Governor said," murmured Zo. "We take no chances."

Out of the corner of his eye, Harry saw Captain Tex's finger tightening on the trigger of the blasters …

"No!" The word was out of his mouth before he could think it through. He ran over and touched Tex's arm. "We can't fire. We don't know who's on board."

"Harry?" said Ava, her voice full of concern. "Are you OK?"

All eyes were on Admiral Achebe. She gave Harry a stern look. "Cadet Hugo. You are not in charge here. Back to your seat, before—"

A crackle sounded over the communicator. A hiss of static, and a woman's voice. A voice Harry knew at once, from recordings he had listened to a thousand times.

"Come in, Tagus. Do you read us? Request permission to come aboard."

Another voice spoke – a man's this time. "We've been held prisoner on Gwildor, but we escaped. Please help us!"

Harry felt dizzy. He turned to Ava and saw that she looked as astonished as he felt himself.

"Harry," she breathed. "Is that …? Could that be …?"

"It's them. It's definitely them." Harry swallowed. "It's Mum and Dad."

CHAPTER 3

SECRETS AND LIES

"Are you absolutely certain, Harry?"
Admiral Achebe gave him a piercing
stare. "If we're wrong about this …"

"He isn't wrong," Zo Harkman said
quietly. His voice trembled with emotion.
"Alanna and Tim Hugo were my best
friends back on Avantia. I'd recognise

their voices anywhere."

Harry saw that his guardian's eyes were glistening with tears, and he felt his own lip quivering.

"Then what are we waiting for?" said Admiral Achebe. "Bring them in."

"Engaging tractor beam," said the pilot. "Readying the airlock."

Harry's heart was beating so hard he thought it might jump out of his chest. He paced the narrow confines of the deck.

"Take it easy, Harry," said Ava, gently. "Why don't you sit down for a minute?"

He just shook his head.

On the viewing screen he could see the pod up close as the tractor beam drew it in: every nick, scrape and dent on its hull. *Any second now I'm going to see them again. Mum. Dad.* All these years he had known they were alive, deep down in his bones. *And I was right.* He could hardly believe it.

CLUNK! The Tagus shuddered as the pod linked up to the external airlock.

Taking one last deep breath, Harry approached the sliding door. Two marines were already waiting on either side, phase rifles shouldered. "Can't be too careful," muttered one of them.

Doubt flashed through Harry's mind for a moment. What if they'd got this all wrong? What if it was all some cruel trick of Vellis's?

There was a hiss of hydraulics and the airlock door rasped open.

It was them. His parents.

They clung to each other, dressed in faded overalls and looking exhausted. His mother was slender and pale with short dark hair and emerald-green eyes. His father was big and broad-shouldered, with a broken nose and spiky silver-blond hair. They stared at him, their eyes wide.

"Mum?" croaked Harry. "Dad?"

Then he flung himself at them and buried his face deep in their clothes. He could feel tears streaming down his face, but at the same time he was laughing, saying their names over and over.

For a long time, they just held him tight.

"Are you OK?" he said at last, when he could finally bring himself to step back and look at them.

Mum nodded. She looked leaner than in the holograms Harry kept back on Vantia1, her face sharper, the lines deeper. But she was all in one piece. Dad too, even if his hair was flecked with grey now. They were alive and well.

"Tim!" said Harkman. "Alanna!" He stepped forward, arms wide for a hug.

Harry's dad just looked at him, eyes glazed.

A pulse of worry shot through Harry. *It's like he doesn't recognise Zo ...* Then his dad cracked a smile and held out a hand.

Harkman shook it, then clasped Harry's mum's hand too. Disappointment flashed across his face, and Harry could tell it wasn't quite the greeting his guardian had been hoping for. *But it's been so long*, he told himself. *It's bound to be different now, isn't it?* Who knew what they'd been through in Vellis's captivity.

"Great to see you again," said Harry's dad. "How long has it been?"

More than eight years, thought Harry. *Since I was a little kid.*

Two more marines approached with blankets and mugs of hot tea. They settled Harry's mum and dad into crash seats. A medic stepped forward.

"Let me examine you," she said.

Harry's dad backed away. "There'll be time for that later."

Harry felt dazed as he stood back, watching it all happen. It still didn't seem real.

Someone laid a hand on his arm, and

he turned to see Ava smiling at him. It made him feel a little steadier to have her there with him.

"How did you escape?" asked Harkman, kneeling beside his old friends.

"By the skin of our teeth," muttered Alanna.

"There was an accident," said Tim. "Vellis got crushed by some mining equipment. He's been extracting Tallium ore."

Harry nodded. "But does that mean he's …"

"Dead?" finished Admiral Achebe. She was peering curiously at their guests from her command chair.

Harry's parents looked at each other,

then nodded. "That's right," said Alanna. "When we found out, we took his personal escape pod."

Harry frowned, rubbing his forehead. "So Vellis is just ... gone?" Somehow, this wasn't the end he had imagined for the evil scientist.

"What was he doing with the Tallium?" asked Harkman.

Tim shrugged. "Whatever it was, he didn't get very far. And luckily for us, we don't have to worry about it any more." He turned his gaze on Harry. "Now we can focus on the future. Our son, Harry ... Look at you! What a fine young lad you've turned out to be!"

Harry grinned.

But at the same time, he felt a squirm of unease. Was it his imagination, or was there something still a little glazed about his father's eyes? As though he were looking straight through him.

"I'm a cadet now," he said. "And this is my best friend, Ava. She's pretty amazing."

"Ah, he's only saying that because I saved his life once or twice," said Ava, giving Harry a wink. "No big deal."

"That's wonderful, Harry," said Harry's mum.

This time, Harry couldn't ignore the nagging feeling of discomfort. His mother hadn't even glanced at Ava.

They're in shock, he reminded himself.

They've been through a terrible ordeal.
Just give them time …

"Let's get you back to Vantia1 straight away," said Harkman, standing. "We need to get a thorough debrief."

"What about the mission?" grunted Tex.

"We should set a course for the surface," added a marine sergeant. "Recover Vellis's body."

"No!"

Alanna's gasp was so loud, it made everyone look at her. "I mean … I don't want to go back to Gwildor. Ever."

Admiral Achebe cleared her throat. "Your objection is noted," she said calmly. "We'll carry out orbital scans as planned and return to Vantia1. If the Governor authorises it, we can return later to find Vellis."

"Plotting a course," said the navigator. The Tagus hummed all around them as the pilot disengaged the escape pod. Then the engines fired, and they slowly moved off once again.

Harry saw his parents' shoulders sag. *After all they've been through ... it's no wonder they don't want to go back!*

"It will be OK," he told them, kneeling at their side. "We're not landing on Gwildor. And you're safe now. I promise."

His dad nodded slowly. "If you say so, Harry. Hey, is there somewhere we can freshen up?"

"The head's that way," said Harkman, pointing to a hatch that led to the lower deck.

As his father climbed down the ladder, Harry noticed Ava beckoning him from the far side of the Tagus. "Give me a hand with this solar shield?"

"Go on," Harry's mum told him. "I'm not going anywhere."

Harry crossed the ship to where Ava was tinkering with a control panel. "What's the matter?" he whispered. "There aren't any solar shields on a Tagus."

"Yeah, I knew that," said Ava, in a low voice. She was tapping distractedly on the control panel, and Harry realised that she was nervous. "I was just thinking … I mean …"

"Spit it out," said Harry.

"Do you feel like there's something a bit … *off* … with your mum and dad?"

The skin prickled at the back of Harry's neck. It was the same thought he'd had himself. "They've been prisoners for a long time," he said, carefully.

"Right. But they don't exactly seem excited to be free, do they?"

"I don't …"

"They didn't seem to know who Zo Harkman was either, and he's supposed to be their best friend."

Harry felt himself flushing with anger. "Who knows what happened to them on

Gwildor? They just need a chance to—"

Suddenly the ship lurched, nearly throwing them off their feet. A groan of metal sounded from somewhere deep in the Tagus's engines.

Harkman darted back to his seat and brought up an engineering display. "Thruster malfunction. One of the power couplings has come loose."

"I'll go," said Harry, before Harkman could assign the job to someone else. He gave Ava a pointed look. "I need to clear my head."

"Wait," said Ava. "I didn't mean to ..."

But Harry had already turned away and was climbing the ladder down below decks. The engine room was lit by strips of blue safety lights. Harry ducked through the doorway, and started. There was someone there already, leaning over the massive bulk of the thrusters.

"Er ... Hello?"

The figure straightened, and Harry saw with a shock that it was his dad. There was that same blank look in his eyes, as though Harry was no more interesting to him than a chair or a lamp. "Hello, son," he said. "I got lost, looking for the bathroom."

Harry tried to smile. "And you thought you'd find it in the main thruster unit?"

"That's right," said Harry's dad, evenly. He was leaning on the engine with one arm, and Harry saw that he was holding something in his hand.

"Hey, is – is that a spanner?" Harry's skin began to prickle all over again.

His dad held up the tool and examined it, looking strangely puzzled. Then his gaze locked on Harry, cold and predatory. "So it is."

He lunged forward, swinging the spanner.

"Whoa!" Harry ducked, stumbled backwards, tripped on a pipe and sprawled on the floor. "Dad, what are you doing?" Confused thoughts tumbled through his mind. *What's happening? Who is this man?*

Because whoever it was, it wasn't his dad.

The man loomed over Harry, throwing a shadow across him. Harry scrambled for the door, but a boot stomped down on his leg, trapping him in place. Then the man dropped the spanner with a *clang*, reached down and locked his big, strong hands around Harry's neck.

"Let ... go ..." gasped Harry. He scrabbled at the man's wrists, trying to prise his hands away. But it was hopeless. The man didn't budge. His fingers began to squeeze, tighter and tighter ...

Harry tried to snatch up the spanner himself, but it was out of reach. Then he remembered. *My laser cutter!* He activated it with the first joint of his robotic middle finger, and a searing beam leapt from the point of his index finger, burning into his attacker's wrist.

There was a shower of sparks, making Harry gasp. The fingers loosened. Then the man jerked away, one hand dangling from his wrist. To his astonishment, Harry saw no blood or bone, just a mess of half-melted cables and metal struts.

"What are you?" he gasped, grabbing the spanner himself.

As his attacker dived for him, he rerouted power to his robotic arm and swung. *CLONK!* The sound the spanner made as it struck the man's head was unnervingly metallic.

As the man who looked like Harry's father slumped to his knees, his eyes began to blink at astonishing speed. His fingers twitched, curling and uncurling. "Nice to meet you, Harry ... Nice to meet you, Harry ... Nice to meet you, Harry," he stuttered.

And now Harry understood. *It's a droid!*

Heart racing, he darted out of the engine room, clambering up the ladder to the main deck. "Ava!" he yelled, sticking his head through the hatch. "Zo!"

"They can't help you," said the woman who looked like his mother.

Harry saw her picking her way towards him, stepping over the bodies of marines who lay sprawled on the floor. Harry felt cold with shock. There was Achebe, slumped in her chair. Ava, curled up next to the control panel. They were all unconscious.

"What have you done to them?" he gasped.

A strange smile spread across the

woman's face. *She's a droid too*, Harry realised.

"Oh, they're only sleeping, Harry. Just like you will be soon."

Harry swallowed hard. "Don't come any closer."

"What's the matter? Don't you want to give your mother a hug?"

She spread her arms wide

and opened her mouth. There was a hissing sound. The sound of gas spilling out. And now Harry could feel it stinging at his nostrils, filling his head. He tried to take a step, but he couldn't feel his legs.

He fell suddenly into darkness.

CHAPTER 4

BREMMER

"Harry? Harry!"

He blinked. Where was he? His head throbbed with pain.

"Hey! Wake up."

A sharp elbow nudged him in the side.

"Ouch," he grumbled. "I'm awake."

He forced his eyes open at last.

Ava was sitting in a crash seat next to him. Beyond, he could see the marines sitting too, all in a row. They were slowly coming round and muttering to each other. Zo Harkman and Achebe were among them, along with the pilot and the navigator. *Everyone's alive ...*

His relief didn't last. Standing opposite, pointing a phase rifle at them with its one remaining hand, was the droid that looked like his father. "Please stay seated," it said.

"Who are you?" snarled Captain Tex. He looked like he might lunge for the droid's throat at any moment.

"Stand down, Captain," said Achebe, quietly. "We don't want casualties."

Harry felt sick to his stomach. How could he have fallen for it? Deep down, he had known there was something not quite right about his "parents", right from the start. Ava had even told him as much. "I'm sorry I didn't listen," he whispered to her. "You were right."

"As usual." Ava tried to smile, but Harry could tell her heart wasn't in it.

Harry saw that the female droid was at the pilot's chair in the cockpit. Beyond, through the viewing screen, something was coming into view. It was a vast, hulking spaceship, drifting in orbit round Gwildor. It dwarfed their Tagus and bristled with weaponry.

They all watched in silence as a

docking bay door slid open in the belly of the craft and the Tagus cruised smoothly through the airlock and into a darkened flight deck. Then there was a *clunk*, and the vessel juddered all around them as they touched down.

"Lock the prisoners in the hold," said the Alanna-droid.

The Tim-droid began to hustle the

marines down below decks. Harry and Ava were just getting to their feet when the female droid's hands fell on their shoulders, pushing them down again. "Not you two."

Harry's mind raced. Could he take on their captors? He didn't have a weapon. And if he tried to fight, they might just knock him out with the sleeping gas again.

"It's not worth it," muttered Ava, as though she had guessed what he was thinking. "You'll get yourself killed."

The Tim-droid emerged at last from below. "Prisoners secure," he said flatly. With a soft click, a barrel emerged from his forearm, then – *whssshhh!* – a length of glowing green cord came whipping out, fast as a snake. Harry barely had time to be surprised before the cord snapped around him, wrapping him in coils that bit into his skin. He squirmed and found that his arms were held tight to his sides.

The Tim-droid tugged hard on the end of the cord. Harry was pulled out of the chair, his knees smacking on to the metal deck. He heard Ava yelp. Out of the corner of his eye he saw that the other droid had her held tight with the same kind of glowing green energy cord.

The exit ramp lowered with a whirr, and the droids dragged Harry and Ava, stumbling, out on to the flight deck.

Lights flickered on and off, as though there had been some kind of electrical failure. The brief glimpses Harry got were of a ship in disrepair, with thick clusters of green mould, or some other alien vegetation, growing across the rusted old walls. He was sweating, he realised. It was hot and humid here, like the Farm Deck where food was grown on Vantia1.

The droids strode ahead, marching side by by side in perfect step with each other.

"Where are they taking us?" whispered Ava, staggering along with her own arms bound, just like Harry.

Harry could only shrug.

They followed winding, poorly lit

corridors, half-consumed by the same strange mould that they had seen on the flight deck. At last they came to a security door, where the Tim-droid slotted an ID card.

The door slid open, and they stepped through into a large control room. *The bridge*. It was just as ramshackle and neglected as the rest of the ship. One console unit was missing an interface and randomly sparking from a severed cable. Two of the giant vid screens that hung overhead were spider-webbed with cracks. Even the vast viewing screen up ahead was smudged and covered in lichen, so that the view of space beyond was mostly obscured.

The command seat was on a raised area in the middle of the bridge. The droids stood aside, allowing Harry and Ava to approach. The chair spun round.

Harry gasped.

A short, middle-aged man sat there, dressed all in black. *Bremmer!* He spread his hands wide and smiled. "Welcome, Cadets Hugo and Achebe, to the *Vengeance.*"

"Traitor," muttered Harry.

Governor Knox's former secretary rose and stepped down from the podium. The lights flickered, revealing him fully for just a moment.

Harry felt an unexpected stab of pity. Bremmer looked like he had lost weight: his clothes hung from him, grubby and unwashed. One arm was bandaged, and his face was sickly pale with hollow eyes. A purple bruise shone on his cheek. *Even his hair looks thinner*, thought Harry.

Had it really been just a few weeks since they had last seen him, smart and healthy, on Vantia1, before he had betrayed them all?

"What happened to you?" asked Ava.

"Wait … Don't tell me that being the servant of an evil maniac turned out to be a bad idea?'

"Funny," snarled Bremmer. He didn't look amused though. "Vellis is a brilliant man. And yes, like many geniuses, he can be … unpredictable." He winced. "I have a feeling he'll be rather happier when he sees his new captives, however."

"So Vellis isn't dead," said Harry.

"Oh, far from it," snorted Bremmer. "He's busier than ever on Gwildor, working on his little project. Meanwhile, I have command of the *Vengeance*. And it seems you have fallen right into my trap."

"*Vellis's* trap," said Ava. "I'm guessing."

A flash of anger crossed Bremmer's

face. "You're in no position to be making smart remarks, Cadet Achebe."

"What about my real parents?" said Harry. "Are they alive too?" His heart was thumping so hard he felt as though it might jump out of his chest.

"Your parents," said Bremmer, narrowing his eyes, "are *essential* for Vellis's plans. Unfortunately they've been rather uncooperative so far. But now we have you, Harry, they may change their tune." He cleared his throat. "Open Gwildor vid-feed, containment unit 4."

There was a hiss, a crackle, then a flickering holographic image materialised overhead. Harry's breath caught. Ava let out a low groan.

It was them this time – *really* them.
They huddled together in the corner of
a metal cell, wrists and ankles shackled
with glowing blue bonds. They looked
frightened, and every bit as haggard and
exhausted as their droid doubles.

Harry heaved at the green cords holding
him captive, but they only tightened.
"Mum! Dad! I'm coming for you – I'm
going to save you!"

Bremmer sniggered as the feed cut out.
"They can't hear you, Harry. You know,
I simply cannot wait to deliver the good
news to my master."

"Don't do this!" said Harry, turning
desperately to Bremmer. "We can help you
get back to Vantia1. Governor Knox will

forgive you … Maybe you won't get your old job back, but you can live safely, with nothing to fear from Vellis."

A strange look came over Bremmer. He opened his mouth, then closed it again. Harry's heart leapt. *He's actually considering it!*

Then Bremmer shook himself and sneered. "A sad little retirement … What a generous offer! And here is Vellis, offering me whole planets to rule. What was I thinking?" He clicked his fingers. "Droids! Take them to the brig."

CHAPTER 5

GWILDOR

The droids marched out into the corridor with Harry and Ava stumbling after them.

Harry squirmed and heaved at his bonds, but the more he struggled, the tighter the glowing green cord became. He flexed his robotic index finger, but that was no good either. *Even if I could activate the laser, I couldn't get it anywhere near the droids!*

Their captors led them off down a ramp on to a lower, darker level of the ship. It was even hotter and more humid here, and Harry's whole uniform was damp with sweat.

"We have to do something," whispered Ava.

Harry bit his lip. If this was one of Zo's old Western films and the heroes were in trouble, the cavalry would show up right at the last minute to save the day. *No such luck.* Unless …

Harry twisted his robotic arm, squeezing it against his hip to activate a button on the wrist module. "The cavalry's coming," he muttered.

Ava looked confused, but as the droids led them round the corner, they suddenly stopped.

Harry could hear it now – the sound which had made the droids pause. A roar of distant engines as something came hurtling through the corridors towards them.

"Wait," said Ava, recognising the noise. "Is that …?"

The Space Stallion screeched around the corner up ahead, thrusters blazing.

"Yee-haw!" whooped the Stallion. *Kachunk!* Its blasters locked into place as it powered towards them.

"Duck!" yelled Harry.

He and Ava dropped down into a crouch just as the blasters let fly. *Thunk-thunk-thunk!* A stream of glowing blue energy bolts slammed into the droids, knocking them off their feet and throwing them hard against the wall with thunderous metallic *clang*s.

The droids slumped to the ground,

smoke spilling from their twisted bodies. They sparked and twitched as their CPUs slowly died.

Harry felt the pressure fade from his arms. When he looked down, he saw the energy cords whip back into the droids' broken launchers.

"Whoa," breathed Ava, rising shakily to her feet. "Not bad."

"Right?" grinned Harry.

"Thank you kindly, partners," said the Space Stallion, touching down next to Harry. "Now, how's about a ride back to the wagon? That is, if y'all don't object to saddling up on a humble ol' hobby-horse."

✪

The heavy door of the hold slid open with a whirr. There was no lighting inside. Harry could only see shadowy shapes as the marines shifted, looking up to see who it was. Then Zo Harkman's ragged voice called from the darkness.

"Harry!"

His guardian came running. The next thing Harry knew, he was wrapped in such a tight hug that he could hardly breathe.

"There's no time!" said Ava. "Mum! Bremmer is on the bridge. He's controlling this ship."

"That lowlife ..." Admiral Achebe stood, drawing herself up with determination in her eyes. "Captain Tex! Bring him to me."

"With pleasure, ma'am."

Harry and Harkman were jostled aside as four of the biggest marines charged out of the hold, armed with phase rifles.

"How did you get away?" asked Zo. He held Harry at arm's length, his eyes shining with pride.

Harry hesitated. "Er … You know how you said not to bring my Space Stallion?"

Harkman's brow furrowed. "Harry, how many times do I have to …" Then he caught himself and smiled. "Well. I suppose just this once I can let it slide."

In a few moments they were all out of the hold and back on the main deck of the Tagus. Achebe and Harkman sat in their command chairs, listening carefully as Harry and Ava explained what they had learned. The Space Stallion hummed quietly, resting against a control panel.

"My parents are alive," said Harry, breathlessly. "And so's Vellis. They're on Gwildor. I know we're only supposed to scan the surface but … well. We have to rescue them, don't we?"

He looked over at Harkman, expecting to see him shaking his head. But to his surprise, his guardian was slowly nodding. "I agree."

"Zo?" said Achebe, raising an eyebrow.

"I know what the Governor's orders were," said Harkman. "But things have changed. Bremmer might have told Vellis that we're here. That means that Tim and Alanna are in danger."

"Exactly!" cried Ava. "What do you say, Mum?"

The Admiral sighed. "Even if we did decide to rescue them, it would be foolish to attempt landing in the Tagus. It's a recon vessel. No heavy armour. Barely a single evasive protocol."

A scuffle sounded outside, boots clanging on the access ramp. Then a pair of marines bundled Bremmer into the spaceship. Captain Tex followed, levelling a phase rifle.

Bremmer collapsed to his knees. "Forgive me!" he begged. "I was just a pawn! I didn't know what I was doing! This ship isn't even mine; I ..." He fell silent as Admiral Achebe raised a hand.

The Admiral frowned. "That gives me an idea ..." she said. "We could take *this* ship. It's old, but if the shield systems are operational, we might stand a chance."

"No!" Bremmer's eyes had gone wide with fear. "Please, you don't understand – Vellis has the best defensive array in the galaxy. You wouldn't even get through the atmosphere. He'll vaporise us!"

"What, even with his loyal friend Bremmer on board?" scoffed Ava.

"Admiral, there's another way," said Harry. He stood aside and pointed to his Space Stallion. Coloured LEDs flashed across the bike's body in a ripple of light.

"You can't be serious," said Harkman sharply. "If Vellis's defences can vaporise a battle cruiser, think what they would do to a simple space bike!"

"Simple?" Harry frowned. "And anyway, he won't vaporise something if he doesn't see it coming. Partner? Make yourself scarce."

Fzoosh! In the blink of an eye, the Stallion was gone.

"What on …?" muttered the Admiral.

"A cloaking device." Harkman slapped his forehead. "Of course. So that's how you got it on board. Hey! Wait!"

Harry was already climbing on to the invisible Stallion. "Vellis won't wait," he said. "And pretty soon he'll figure out that we've got Bremmer. Then *all* our lives will be in danger."

"I'll open the airlock," said Ava. She darted down the access ramp.

"Young lady!" said her mother. "Do not even think about—"

Harry twisted the throttle. *Vrrrooomm!*

The roar of the thrusters was deafening in the enclosed space of the Tagus. Even the marines ducked low, clapping their hands over the ears.

The Stallion jolted forward as Harry heaved at the handlebars. He pulled up, clearing the heads of the marines, and shot out on to the flight deck.

Ava was already waiting by the airlock as it slowly opened. The red light above it turned green, and a siren wailed.

Harry slowed, feeling the Stallion

judder as Ava leapt on to it behind him. She had found a phase rifle somewhere, and had it strapped over her shoulder.

"Activate skins!" yelled Harry. He pressed a button on his belt buckle, and the space-skin inflated from his uniform, covering his hands and head in transparent protective material.

Behind him he could hear marines running out on to the deck; Achebe calling for Ava; Harkman shouting Harry's name …

"Sorry!" he called back. But his cry was lost beneath the roar of the engines.

Then they were gone, speeding out into the endless blackness of space.

CHAPTER 6

CRUSHER

Harry leaned hard to the right, throwing them into a corkscrew. Over the intercom, he heard Ava chuckling behind him.

Far below, Gwildor hung in the endless darkness of space. It looked huge from here, dwarfing the rocky

red-grey sphere of Avantia that lay beyond. But Harry knew that, in reality, Avantia's moon was far smaller than the planet it orbited – barely five hundred kilometres in diameter.

"Scanning," said the Stallion calmly, as they descended. "No atmosphere down there, partners. Best keep them skins activated. Gravity looks fine and dandy though."

Harry crouched down low, feeling winds rushing over him as they hurtled closer. Gwildor looked barren and craggy, a wasteland of reddish rock and sand.

"See that?" said Ava, pointing over Harry's shoulder.

A network of trenches was cut into the rocky surface of Gwildor. They were hundreds of miles long, winding and spreading out like a spider's web from a cluster of colossal industrial buildings.

"That has to be Vellis's mining operation," said Harry. He let out a low whistle. "He must have collected mega-tonnes of Tallium already."

He pulled up, leaving his stomach behind. As he cut the throttle, he steered the Stallion towards a central trench, close to the industrial buildings.

"Cloaking device seems to have fooled Vellis's scanners," said Ava.

"So far," muttered Harry.

Up close, they saw how wide and deep the trenches were – as big as ravines.

"Pickin' up high Tallium radiation levels," said the Space Stallion.

Harry banked, bringing the Stallion down inside a trench. As they sailed past the craggy red rock walls, they could see tunnel entrances at ground level, leading off towards the base in the centre. The Stallion's landing gear engaged with a *clunk*, and the bike jolted as they touched down.

"Thanks, buddy," said Harry, patting the Stallion's flank.

"Where now?" asked Ava, looking all around. The bottom of the trench was rugged and uneven, strewn with broken bits of rock. The high walls were just as barren and featureless. Overhead, the sky was black and pricked with stars.

"Do you feel that?" asked Harry. Ava nodded. The ground shuddered beneath them, as though they had landed in the middle of a low-level earthquake.

"Somethin's comin'," observed the Space Stallion.

The shudders were coming at regular

intervals, Harry realised. *Is it a machine?*

"Take cover," hissed Harry. He grabbed Ava by the arm and pulled her down behind a boulder. Then he peered up above it, just as the source of the earthquakes came into view.

His breath caught in his throat.

It was a vast, monstrous creature, almost the size of a battle cruiser. Its bulk seemed to fill the whole width and depth of the trench. But that wasn't what was most extraordinary about it.

"It's a ... *dog*," gasped Ava.

"With *three heads*," added Harry.

The massive droid prowled forward, shaking the ground and sending up clouds of rock-dust with each step.

Savage, razor-sharp gold claws protruded from its paws. Its teeth looked even more deadly, translucent chunks of some synthetic material. Its armour plating was blood-red and grey, and in the gaps between Harry could see bunched cables running like robotic sinews.

The monster's six eyes glowed with a pitiless, icy blue light.

The dog-droid lowered one of its heads. Its neck extended, like a concertina, and its jaws dug deep into the bottom of the trench.

Harry could feel the ground trembling beneath him once again as the monster chewed up the solid rocks like dog biscuits and swallowed, the boulders tumbling into the creature's belly.

"So it's a guard dog *and* a mining bot?" breathed Ava.

A chute lowered from the droid's belly, and a silver cartridge the size of a transport pod was ejected, sliding down among the rocks. The chute swivelled round, and a tide of scree came scraping down afterwards. *Waste product*, Harry guessed. *The Tallium ore must be in the silver cartridge.*

Before they could get a closer look, the droid set off again, prowling towards them. Its mouths clicked open to reveal massive torches that swept the floor and walls of the trench like searchlights …

"Hide!" yelped Ava. This time it was

she who grabbed Harry by the arm and tugged him away from the boulder. They ducked into one of the side tunnels and flattened themselves against the rocky walls. Then they held their breath, motionless, as the droid passed on by.

It took a while for the vibrations of the droid's steps to die away, and for the rock-dust to settle in its wake.

"Phew …" gasped Harry, at last. He peered into the darkness of the tunnel. "Hey, this leads towards the refinery buildings, remember?"

Ava nodded. "Ten to one, that's where your parents are."

They set out, creeping cautiously through the narrow passage. But they'd hardly taken ten steps when something glinted up ahead. Something moving.

Adrenaline surged through Harry all over again. "What is that?"

Ava didn't reply – just raised her phase rifle. The power chamber glowed blue as it charged, ready to fire.

Then, out of the darkness, came another droid. It was a mechanised six-legged bot, nothing like the sleek dog creature they had just seen. It was no bigger than Harry's Space Stallion, and it was constructed in the form of an ant. All the hydraulics and wires were exposed, the legs scissoring up and down like pistons.

It was charging straight at them.

CHAPTER 7

DESTROYER OF WORLDS

"Stay back or I shoot!" shouted Ava.

The droid didn't react. It just kept on scuttling up the tunnel.

Harry frowned. Now that the droid was out of the shadows, he could see its head array more clearly. The sensors were primitive at best. *Maybe not smart enough to detect a life form.*

"I'm warning you!" hissed Ava. She closed one eye, sighting down the phase rifle.

"Wait." Harry took her by the arm and pulled her to the side of the tunnel. "Just watch," he whispered.

They froze, tense, as the droid scrabbed over the rocks, not altering its course in the slightest.

Harry relaxed. "I figured. It can't tell we're here," he explained. "It's not like Vellis's other droids. It's got no more sentience than a vacuum cleaner."

"Some vacuum cleaner," said Ava, with a shudder, as the giant robotic insect passed by, pistons plunging up and down. "Hey – here comes another."

Sure enough, a second, then a third ant-droid came jerking towards them. They clambered past Harry and Ava, out into the huge trench, and picked their way across the rocks until they reached the silver cartridges left behind by the massive dog-droid.

Harry watched one of the ant-droids as it used its front legs like a forklift, raising the silver cartridge, then carrying it back into the tunnel.

"They're taking the Tallium ore back to the refinery," he said.

"So if we follow them …" added Ava.

Harry nodded. "They might lead us to Vellis."

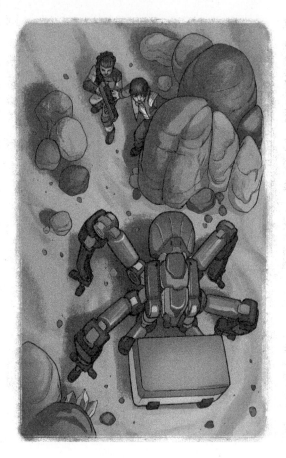

The last
of the ants
returned to
the tunnel,
and Harry
and Ava fell
in behind
it, edging
their way
into the
darkness.
Harry
activated a torch set into the wrist unit
on his robotic arm, and the glow lit up
rugged rocks all around them. They
hurried, but couldn't keep up with the
ants. Soon though, the tunnel became

lighter, until Harry was able to switch off the torch.

Then at last they turned a corner and came to a circular metal gateway.

As they stepped through, Harry felt a faint tugging at his body. *A force field?* He could hear noises now. A cacophony of humming, clanking and whirring fans. *Some sort of factory ...*

His suit beeped, and a green light flashed under the face shield.

"There's an artificial atmosphere in here," he told Ava. "We can deactivate skins."

But she wasn't listening. "Whoa ..." she breathed, gazing all around.

They were standing in a huge,

brightly lit space that reminded Harry
of the flight deck back on Vantia1. The
opposite wall was entirely taken up by
a towering silver unit with hundreds
of octagonal holes in it, like a massive
honeycomb. To their right, the ants
were clattering up a flight of metal
stairs to a gantry running parallel to
the honeycomb wall. There, each ant
lowered the silver capsule it carried
into the waiting arms of an articulated
gripper. With a buzz and a whirr, the
gripper sped away, carrying the capsule
with it, rotating and slotting it neatly
into the silver wall.

Harry watched, open-mouthed.

With a soft *thunk*, each capsule was

emptied into some waiting receptacle on the far side. Then the gripper removed the capsule, carried it down to the bottom of the wall and deposited it gently on a conveyor belt that ran below. At the end of the belt, Harry saw a squad of basic industrial droids on caterpillar treads waiting to ferry the empty capsules away.

For a few moments, they could only watch in silent astonishment. Vellis's operation was huge!

Ava nudged him and gestured with her phase rifle. Following her gaze, Harry spotted a circular control room suspended from the ceiling, with viewing windows running all around it.

There was another flight of metal stairs leading up from the gantry. Together, they darted to the stairs and took them two at a time. The ants had already disappeared through a security door, and Harry couldn't see any guards. *Some good luck, for once ...* Vellis probably wasn't counting on anyone making it to the surface of Gwildor, let alone into his refinery.

They took the second flight of stairs and pushed through a set of swinging doors into the control room.

Like the ant-droids, everything here was built to be functional. Most of the consoles didn't even have any housings, just exposed circuitry and wiring. Several monitors bleeped softly, stats and measurements scrolling endless across the screens. There were a couple of battered old swivel chairs and a plinth in the centre – a projection table, just like the one in Harkman's lab.

There must have been some soundproofing, because it was much quieter in here than on the refinery floor. So quiet it gave Harry a shiver down the back of his spine. *Where's Vellis? Is there nobody here at all?*

"I don't understand," said Ava, frowning. "What's all of this *for*?"

"Let's take a look." Harry crossed to the main control console and got to work, accessing the most recent files.

An image flickered into life above the projection table, spinning in three dimensions and constructed of soft, glowing green lines. Reams of equations, schematics and formulae scrolled next to it, with close-up diagrams of different parts of the model cycling past.

"Uh oh ..." said Ava.

Harry's breath caught as he stared at the image. He didn't know what it was – not exactly. But from the mounting, the power conduits and the massive bore of the barrel, it wasn't hard to guess.

"It's a weapon," he croaked. "Vellis is building a *weapon*."

Ava looked as though she was about to say something ... Then her eyes widened.

She dropped suddenly into a crouch and brought her phase rifle to her shoulder, aiming at the door.

Harry froze. He could hear it now too. *Voices.* Someone was coming.

Quickly, he ducked down behind the projection table, out of view. Ava crept over to join him, still covering the door with her rifle.

Footsteps, clanging on the metal stairs. Then the doors swung open and two figures entered, dressed in bulky black hazmat suits. Harry watched, peering around the edge of the projection table.

"I've been very patient, you know. Too patient."

Vellis's voice. But, to Harry's surprise, it wasn't one of the figures who spoke. The voice came from a metal orb, no bigger than a Zero-G handball. It floated above the figures, rotating slowly, with a camera embedded in it. *Like an eye, watching them.*

"I think I deserve to see some progress," said the orb. "After all, I'd hate to have to shoot the boy out into space. How long do you think he'd last out there, with no oxygen?"

"We're working as fast as we can," said one of the figures. A man. He sounded desperate.

At his voice, Harry's stomach squirmed.

"Well, you'll just have to work faster then, won't you?" said Vellis. And with a soft electronic whine, the orb flew out of the room.

"He's bluffing," said the other figure. But her voice trembled.

"We can't take that risk. There must be some way to speed things up …" The man sighed and pulled off the helmet of his hazmat suit. The woman did the same.

All the breath left Harry's body. He felt dizzy, like he might faint on the spot.

It was them. It was *really* them. They had the same haggard faces as the fake droids, the same sad eyes, dark-ringed with anxiety. The same weary sag of the shoulders.

But this time it wasn't a trick.

Harry felt Ava's hand close on his arm. *Careful*, she mouthed.

But Harry couldn't help himself.

"Don't scream," he said out loud. "Don't say a word." He stood, his legs shaking.

The man and the

woman turned to meet his gaze.

For a little while the three of them just stood, staring at each other. Harry half-wished the moment would never end.

At last the woman spoke. "Harry? Is it … is it you?"

Then the spell was broken, and Harry threw himself into the arms of his sobbing parents.

CHAPTER 8

GUARD DOG

"Harry ..." **His** father's eyes were swollen and glistening with tears. "I can't tell you what it means to ... to see you after ..." He faltered, swallowing hard.

"It's OK, Dad." Harry wrapped him up in another tight hug. He couldn't stop touching them. He was afraid that if he let go, they might somehow turn out not to be real.

But they were real. He knew it deep down in his bones. Flesh and blood. This time it was no trick of Vellis's.

My parents are alive. We're a family again. He could still barely believe it.

His mother joined the embrace, and they clung to each other.

Harry tried to fix the moment in his mind. The warmth and softness of their bodies, the beating of their hearts and the smell of them, so strange and yet so familiar.

It felt like coming home after a lifetime in the cold.

At last they came apart, and Harry noticed Ava hovering in the background, looking awkwardly at her feet.

"Mum? Dad?" he said, wiping away his own tears. "This is my friend Ava. My *best* friend."

Ava held out a hand cautiously, but Harry's mum brushed it aside and swept Ava up into a hug too. "It's so good to meet you," she said.

Harry saw a smile spread across Ava's face. "You too, Mrs Hugo."

"Call me Alanna."

Harry grinned at his dad. But anxiety had clouded Tim Hugo's face. "Harry, we must get out of here. If Vellis finds us, I don't know what he'll do."

"Don't worry, Dad," said Harry. He felt a tingle run through him, just at using the word *Dad*. "We've faced Vellis before. We've beaten him too."

"You don't understand," said his mum, gravely. She stepped back from Ava and gestured to the spinning projection. "This *thing* that Vellis is making us build ... it's almost ready."

"It's a Tallium ray," said Harry's dad. "It

can destroy a space station in an instant.
Even a small planet. When it's finished,
it will be the deadliest weapon in the
galaxy." He paused, staring at Harry.
"Why are you smiling?"

"You said *when* it's finished," said
Harry. "Until then, there's still hope."

"That's my boy," said his mum, quietly.

His dad nodded. "Right. The Tallium is
dangerously unstable. That means Vellis
can't actually move the weapon. Not yet,
anyway. That's what we're working on."

"Well, that ends now," said Ava. "We're
going to get you off this moon."

Harry's mum smiled sadly. "That won't
be easy, I'm afraid. There are no escape
pods in the refinery. Vellis has a few ships

at his private base, but ..."

"The base is somewhere else?" asked Harry.

"Twenty miles north-west of here," said his dad. "But he has Eyes all over the refinery – they're spying devices."

"Like that hovering orb we saw earlier, you mean?" said Ava.

"That's right," said Tim. "No way we can escape without being spotted."

"I wouldn't be so sure," said Harry.

"You've got an idea?" asked his mum.

Harry nodded. "I think there's a way we can sneak out of here without it spotting us. Listen to me ..."

✪

Harry shifted, wrapping his arms and legs

tighter around the metal body of the ant. His muscles burned with the effort of clinging on. *This is harder than I'd thought!*

If he craned his neck, he could just see his mum up ahead, holding on tight to the underside of the ant in front. Dad and Ava were behind him, each carried along in the same way by one of the industrial droids.

Harry's droid jolted him up and down, its legs scrabbling at the rocks. It felt as though they'd been going down this tunnel for ever. *It would be so much easier if we could just ride on the ants' backs!* But it was too risky. His dad wasn't sure how many "Eyes" Vellis had. If even one of the spying devices spotted them it would spell disaster, so they had to stay hidden from view.

At last light spilled in from the tunnel entrance, and the ants scurried out into the open air. Harry dropped down, landing among the rocks. His ant carried on without even noticing, heading off to collect another cartridge left behind in the trench by the giant dog-droid.

"Nice work, Harry," said his dad, picking himself up and dusting himself off. His mum and Ava were already on their feet. "But now what? How are we going to get to Vellis's base?"

"No problem," said Harry. "Just watch."

He tapped at the forearm panel on his

robotic arm. A moment later, his Space Stallion shimmered into view a metre away, right behind the rock where they had left it. "Howdy, partners," it said.

Harry's mum gasped. "Is that yours, Harry?"

"Built it myself," said Harry proudly.

"And he won't stop going on about it," said Ava, nudging him. But she was grinning all the same.

Harry's dad ran a hand over the chrome bodywork, checking the controls, the thrusters and the electrics. "Harry, this is … amazing."

Harry felt his cheeks heating up. "It's nothing," he mumbled, suddenly embarrassed. He cleared his throat. "It won't carry all of us off this moon, but a short trip to Vellis's base should be OK."

"You're full of surprises, Harry," said his mum, with a smile.

Still blushing, Harry took the handlebars and Ava climbed on behind. He could feel the bike sinking lower as his parents squeezed on too. "Can you handle the extra baggage, buddy?" he asked the Stallion. He hadn't designed it to carry two people, let alone four.

"Only one way to find out, partner."

Harry nodded. And he was just about to twist the throttle when Ava spoke from behind. "Hey. Do you feel that?"

They all waited, silent. Then Harry did feel it – the bike shuddering beneath him. A moment later, another shudder. It felt horribly familiar.

"It's coming!" gasped Harry's mum.

"Kerbrus," breathed his dad. They had both gone very pale.

No time to lose!

Harry gunned the engines and they shot off, climbing towards the top of the trench. He could feel the Stallion straining to carry the extra load.

Glancing back, he saw the three massive heads of the dog-droid come snaking round the corner of the trench, jaws gaping wide.

"Well, hello there," said the voice of Vellis, over Harry's comms. "And where do you think you're going?"

CHAPTER 9

BATTLE ON THE SANDS

"Hold on!" roared Harry, and he pulled the bike into a hard left. Wind whistled past as one of the giant dog heads snapped its jaws centimetres above him.

He banked, firing the thrusters on full power. Above, he saw the edge of the trench. *If we can just get over the top* ...

"Incoming!" shouted Harry's mum.

He swerved away again as a missile streaked past, and an explosion bloomed bright orange against the wall of the trench, showering rubble down below. Harry felt a wave of heat wash over him, and he tightened his grip on the handlebars.

Vellis laughed. "What's the matter, Harry? Surprised my guard dog can bark as well as bite?"

A second missile came whooshing in, and this time Harry jinked aside only just in time. It exploded on the trench floor, far below. He wondered where Vellis was controlling Kerbrus from – it might be possible to block the signal.

Hammering the turbo boost, Harry drove the bike at last over the lip of the trench. *Made it!* He levelled off. Ahead, the dusty red rocks stretched out in an endless plateau.

"There!" called Harry's dad, pointing over his shoulder. "Vellis's base."

Squinting, Harry could just make out a glinting cluster of transparent dome pods in the distance. "Got it." He crouched low, streaking across the desert without slowing for a moment.

"Harry!" Ava's cry drew his attention. He threw a glance over his shoulder, and his blood froze.

Kerbrus was clambering out of the

trench, heaving its way up on to the plateau using its massive hydraulic-powered legs, its three heads rearing wildly like snakes.

"No way ..." breathed Harry.

Three missiles launched from three open mouths, smoke trails pluming behind them as they screeched straight towards the Stallion.

Harry dodged. The lead missile slammed into the ground like a fist, throwing up a cloud of red dust that swirled around them.

Then came a second explosion, horrifyingly close, blindingly bright. The bike spun suddenly out of control. Smoke spilled from its side, stinging Harry's eyes and nostrils.

"D-d-direct hit," stuttered the Stallion. "D-direct hit ..."

Harry heaved at the bars, but it was hopeless. The bike spun again and again. Harry felt the bars torn from his hands, his legs left the saddle, and – *whump!* – he smacked into something.

He sat up, dazed, as the smoke and dust cleared. His back ached from the impact with the sand dune.

Glancing round, he felt a rush of relief. His mum was helping his dad to get up. Ava was already dusting herself off.

The Stallion was half buried in sand, its back thrusters still firing weakly. Harry ran to shut off the engine. A quick check told him that it was still operational, and relief washed over him a second time.

But from behind he could feel the great stomping strides of the dog-droid, shaking the earth and throwing up dust as it closed on them.

"Is everyone OK?" asked Harry.

"All good," called Ava. "Wait. Oh no …"

She was pointing to the back of Harry's mum's suit. With a stab of alarm, Harry saw a long rip in the fabric.

"Mum!" He ran to her. "Mum, your suit's damaged."

She waved him aside impatiently. "It's fine. Emergency oxygen will kick in."

"But that will only give you a few minutes." Harry's dad looked desperately pale beneath his helmet. "We have to get her inside."

Harry shielded his gaze, peering over towards Vellis's base. They were close now, no more than a few hundred metres. Then he looked back and saw the towering dog-droid, still advancing like some terrifying robotic war machine.

His heart thumped loudly in his ears.

"It'll catch us before we get there," he muttered. "Unless …" He turned to his parents. "You go on. We'll hold it up."

"No!" Harry's mum's eyes were wide. "We can't lose you, Harry, not after—"

"Please." Harry held her hands tightly. "It's the only way. I can handle it."

His mum opened her mouth as if to speak, then closed it again. Harry could see the indecision flickering in her eyes.

"Our boy's right," said Harry's dad, quietly. He laid a hand on Harry's shoulder. "Just promise us. Promise us you'll come back alive."

"I promise." Harry tried not to let his voice shake.

He watched them go, stumbling across the rocks, clinging on to each other for support. *I won't lose you*, he silently swore. *Never again.*

"What's the plan, Harry?" said Ava.

Harry turned to her, and the fierce set of her jaw fired him with a new determination. "You take the Space Stallion," he said, hauling the bike free from the sand and activating it again. "Keep Kerbrus busy."

"On it." Ava tossed him the phase rifle. She was already mounted up by the time he caught it. With a flick of her wrist, the thrusters flamed blue and she shot off, streaking through the dark sky towards the monstrous canine robot.

Harry watched, holding his breath, as she drove the Stallion closer to the dog-droid. A neck ratcheted out and jaws snapped at Ava. Harry's heart jolted, but there was no need to worry – she had already darted out of range.

Then he noticed something. The other two dog-heads were staring straight at him, searchlights glaring from their open mouths. And with a rumble, the dog-droid began to run, taking huge, loping strides and eating up the ground between them.

Ava looped round, but Kerbrus had lost interest in her. And now Vellis's voice murmured in Harry's ears. "I'm coming for you, Harry ..."

Heart thumping, he turned and ran. He charged the phase rifle and fired over his shoulder, without looking. He stumbled over a rock, regained his balance and ran on. But within moments he was panting. His feet sank deep in the soft sand. He couldn't seem to get up any speed.

He could feel the dog-droid behind him, still galloping thunderously. He couldn't resist one glance over his shoulder and—

His foot hit a rock. He sprawled face first, trapping the rifle beneath him. He scrambled upright, but already a shadow had fallen on him.

Looking up, Harry saw Kerbrus towering, one paw raised to stomp down on him. He froze, unable to move. Unable to think.

Whoa! A rocket smacked into one of the monster's heads, exploding in a shower of blue sparks. The dog-droid lost its footing and staggered sideways. The paw that had been about to crush Harry thudded down, sending up a harmless spray of sand not ten metres away.

A phase rocket ... Harry spotted Ava speeding away on the Space Stallion, its launchers smoking. "Yee-ha!" whooped the Stallion. "Well, don't just stand there, partner!"

Harry snapped out of it. Aiming the phase rifle, he let fly. A stream of blue energy bolts hit the dog-droid. They pattered off, as harmless as pebbles on a metal sheet.

No use blasting it apart ... but maybe there's another way!

Dropping the rifle, he took aim again, but this time with his robotic arm. The grappling hook shot from its housing, juddering his arm as the high-tensile cable unspooled. The hook snagged at the base of Kerbrus's necks and the cable whipped tight, jerking Harry towards the monster.

Activating another control, Harry set the winch in motion. For a second, his boots skidded across the sand. Then he was airborne, swinging from the cable as it pulled him up. As he was lifted higher, his body slammed against the dog-droid's metal armour. He reached with his free hand, hoping for something to hold on to, but there was nothing.

Then – *whump* – he reached the

grappling hook. Disengaging it, he clambered up on to the dog-droid's back, lying as flat as he could so he wouldn't slide off.

Kerbrus bucked, trying to throw him, but he clung on with all his strength.

If he could get at the monster's inner workings, maybe he could find a way to disable it. *But how?* He hadn't even made a dent in the armour with his phase rifle. And he didn't know how long he could hang on.

Then he saw something.

Smoke billowed from the head that Ava's rocket had hit. It was a mess of twisted and blackened metal. Its neck seemed frozen in place, curving slightly upwards, and its jaws hung open, lifeless.

A way in!

All he had to do was crawl right into the jaws of the beast …

CHAPTER 10

VENGEANCE

One of the monster's other heads was curving back on itself, snaking towards Harry like a sea serpent. Its teeth glinted as the dog's jaws gaped wide, ready to snap at him.

That's my cue ...

Hauling himself into a crouch, Harry

leapt forward. His robotic arm smacked against the neck of the destroyed head as he straddled it, arms and legs spread wide. The neck was segmented, providing plenty of handholds. Harry heaved himself upwards, climbing it like a ladder, as fast as he could. Smoke was still seeping from the wrecked head.

With luck, that means Kerbrus can't see me either.

Soon he could only feel his way. He pulled himself up by one of the monster's ears, crawled along its snout and swung himself down into the mouth of the beast. There was less smoke inside, and he could make out the gaping darkness of the dog's throat, the cavernous roof of its mouth and the huge metal tongue he was standing on. At any moment, the jaws might snap shut …

Ignoring his every instinct, Harry crept deeper into the droid's mouth. Beyond the tongue, lodged in the throat, he came across giant grinding gears with savage metal teeth. *The rock crushing mechanism*, he realised. His heart beat even faster as he slid between the gears. If they started up now, he was finished.

He was just lowering himself through when his boot slipped on the smooth metal inside the droid's throat. His stomach lurched.

"Whoa!" He floundered, throwing his

arms out for purchase. But the throat was too wide. And now he was falling, sliding down the throat like it was a water chute. Every scrape and bang of his elbows and knees clanged and echoed in the enclosed space …

Thump. He landed, pain jarring through his back. Battered and bruised, Harry groggily rose to his feet.

The throat had led to a large, dome-shaped chamber that had to be within the dog-droid's chest cavity. Looking to his left, Harry saw two other tunnel entrances leading off it. *The other two necks*, he thought. Overhead, the walls of the chamber were covered in huge screens that showed a number

of different camera angles, all around
the droid. He saw Ava flick past on one
screen, still riding the Space Stallion. But
why were there monitors inside a mining
droid? Unless this wasn't just a mining
droid …

A voice sounded from the centre of
the chamber. A voice that chilled Harry's
blood.

"So here you are, at last. You know,
I've been so looking forward to meeting
you in person, Harry."

Turning slowly, Harry took in the sight
before him.

In the middle of the metal floor
was a smaller dome formed of some
strange, transparent blue light. Inside it

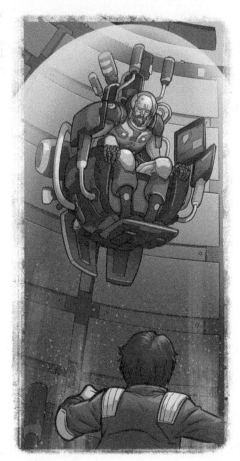

was a hovering command chair with a bank of controls built into it, like a vast metal throne. And sitting in the chair …

Harry's hands balled into fists. So Vellis wasn't controlling the droid remotely, after all. He was right here.

His enemy looked a shadow of his former self. His muscles were withered, his hair all fallen out and his cheeks were sunken, so that his head looked little more than a skull. His skin was pale and sallow.

Only his ice-blue eyes were unchanged. They blazed with a familiar, fierce arrogance.

Vellis's thin lips curled into a sneer. "Did you miss me?"

A ragged cry of rage slipped out of Harry, and before he could think, he had hurled himself across the chamber.

Ffffzzaaap!

Electricity jolted through him. He staggered back. His muscles burned, all the energy drained from them in an instant. He sank to his knees.

"One of my little inventions," smirked

Vellis, indicating the dome of blue light that surrounded him. "Just a precaution, you understand. I know you have a bit of a temper, Harry." He cocked his head. "You look well."

"You look … terrible," grunted Harry. His body still throbbed with pain from the electric shock.

Up close, he could see tubes running from Vellis's nose into his body suit. The suit was black and bulky with wires, armour plates and pouches of some fluorescent blue liquid. Medicine, he guessed.

"What happened to you?" said Harry. He could feel the strength starting to return to his limbs. *If I can just play for*

*time, maybe I can figure out how to get
to him!*

"Oh, this?" said Vellis, looking down at
his suit. He waved a hand dismissively.
"You of all people should know, Harry,
that appearances can be deceptive. I'm
stronger than ever."

"I doubt that," muttered Harry,
through gritted teeth. "You look like
you're wasting away. It's the Tallium, isn't
it?"

"Yes, it seems it can be rather
dangerous," said Vellis, with a sigh.
"Something that you and everyone you
love will discover, just as soon as my little
project is completed."

Harry's legs still felt shaky, but he

managed to stand. "You mean your Tallium ray? That's all over, Vellis. My parents are done helping you. And you're not smart enough to figure out how to move it by yourself, are you?"

Vellis snorted with laughter. "Your concern is really very touching. But don't worry about my project. Worry about your parents. I'm afraid I don't have much patience for those who betray me."

He pressed a button on his armrest, and every screen in the chamber flickered to show a single image. It was a view from one of the dog-droid's heads, magnified several times to show Harry's parents, stumbling across the sands.

They hadn't reached Vellis's base yet.

The floor pitched suddenly, making Harry stumble. The chamber was rumbling all around, and Harry had to drop to a crouch to keep his balance. *We're moving!* And now he saw his parents getting bigger and bigger on the screen, as the dog-droid thundered towards them.

"Say goodbye to your mother and father, Harry!" cackled Vellis. He had one hand on a joystick which was thrust fully forwards. "They're about to become a dog's dinner!"

Harry engaged the comms device on his space skin. "Ava? Come in, Ava!"

"I read you, Harry," Her voice crackled

back at him. "I'm with you, but my blasters are down."

Harry cursed silently. "What about the phase rockets?"

"Only one left."

Harry shot a glance at Vellis, safe within his protective blue shield, still holding the joystick forward. If he didn't do something now, his parents would pay the price.

Worth another shot.

He charged at Vellis a second time, holding up his robotic arm in the hope of breaking the shield.

Fffzzzapp!

The electricity hit him again like a freight ship, slamming him back down on the ground.

Vellis just laughed. "Enjoy the show, Harry," he said. "Because there's nothing you can do to stop it."

Harry shook himself, trying to get the dizziness out of his head. *He's right. No way to stop it. Unless …*

"Ava," he croaked. "Aim for the legs."

"You sure?" came her voice. "I've only got one chance—"

"And we've got to take it," Harry cut in.

"Give up, Harry," snarled Vellis. "Have you seen the size of my droid? There's no way your puny little Stallion can—"

BOOOM!

The chamber shuddered, the explosion ringing out from somewhere below. There was a jolt, and suddenly they weren't moving any more.

"Bull's eye!" whooped Ava, over the comms.

"What?" snapped Vellis. "What's happening?"

A smile spread across Harry's face. Then he froze.

Slowly but surely, he could feel the

floor of the chamber start to tip. He was sliding now, scrabbling for something to hold onto. But it was no use – he smacked into the far wall. "We're going over!" he yelled.

Vellis yanked at the controls, cursed and slammed a fist down on an array of buttons. But Harry could tell it was hopeless. Kerbrus must have lost a leg … and now it was tipping over.

With a deafening *CRASH*, they smashed on to the rocky desert floor, then – *bang!*

Everything went black.

11

COUNTDOWN

*"**Critical damage** ... critical damage
... critical damage ..."*

Harry blinked. *Must have hit
something.* His head ached like crazy. But
at least that meant he was still alive.

A wailing siren was sounding over
the robotic voice of the damage report.

Kerbrus must still have been lying on its side, because the chamber was at ninety degrees, with Harry huddled against one wall.

How long was I out for? Just a few seconds, it looked like.

The control chamber was in chaos. Screens crackled, fizzing with static and spraying out sparks. The blue dome that had protected Vellis flickered, malfunctioning in some serious way.

Vellis himself was gone.

Harry felt a rush of frustration. Then he heard a groan from behind.

Turning, he saw Vellis's heavy command chair lying on its side next to him. It must have fallen right through the protective dome, the anti-grav thrusters busted beyond repair.

He stepped around the chair. And there was his enemy, still strapped in, eyes half-closed. A trickle of blood oozed from one nostril.

Harry felt strangely weary. "It's over," he said. "Just come quietly, Vellis. There'll be a fair trial for you on Vantia1."

Vellis made a strange noise. At first Harry feared he was choking. Then he realised it was a wet, sneering chuckle.

"Oh, it's certainly over, Harry," Vellis croaked. "But not for me."

The straps disengaged, and Vellis stood suddenly, hidden hydraulics hissing in his body suit to raise him artificially to his feet.

Harry stepped back, raising the laser cutter on his robotic finger. "Stay put," he warned.

"I don't think so." Vellis held out one gloved hand, and Harry saw something nestled in his palm. It was a small remote control device, with a glowing red button in the centre. "This is a detonator," said Vellis. "Wired up to the Tallium reactor. You see, Harry? I'm afraid I will always be one step ahead of you. One press of this button, and the reactor blows. It'll take the whole moon with it. Anyone within a fifty-kilometre orbit too, so you can say goodbye to your friends up there. You'll all be space dust."

Harry licked his lips. His hand was trembling, but he managed to hold it still. "You're bluffing."

"Am I?" A horrible smile spread across Vellis's face. "You have been a worthy adversary, Harry. I'll give you that. But you'll never beat me. You simply don't have that ... killer instinct."

Using the toecap of his boot, Vellis tapped a button on the control panel of his chair.

Ker-chunk! The top of the dome broke off and fell away, revealing the red sandy desert and black, star-speckled sky overhead.

When Harry looked back, he saw that Vellis had engaged his space skin, and jets had clicked into place at the side of his boots. Now they fired blue, lifting Vellis slowly up into mid-air.

Harry gritted his teeth. He so desperately wanted to fire, but he knew

he couldn't risk it. "I'll find you," he promised. "I'll bring you to justice."

"You'd have to get off Gwildor alive first," said

Vellis, mockingly. "I have to say, I don't fancy your chances." Holding up the detonator, he pressed the button and tossed it to Harry.

Harry's stomach plummeted as he caught it. A countdown was already running on a small screen, in glowing red digits.

Five minutes to detonation ...

He looked up, but Vellis really was gone this time. He streaked out across the desert, flying low, until all Harry could see of him were the twin blue dots of his rocket boots still firing.

We have to get out of here!

Tucking the detonator in a pocket, Harry clambered out of the wreckage of the dog-droid. Shielding his gaze, he scanned the horizon until he saw something – a pod soaring up into space from the north-west. *My parents!* Relief flooded his body. *At least they made it.*

He engaged the comms on his space skin, connecting to the Tagus.

"Zo? Admiral?"

"Harry? Where are you? What in the name of Avantia is going on down there?" His guardian's voice was tight with anger. It was still a relief to hear it.

"No time to explain. There's a pod coming to you. My parents are on board – my *real* parents. As soon as they're with you, head straight back to Vantia1, full speed."

"What the—"

But Harry killed the comms before he could hear any more.

Ava came swooping down on the Space Stallion. "Nice shot, huh?" But her look of triumph disappeared as she saw Harry's own expression. "Wait – what's the matter?"

"Vellis got away," said Harry. "And he's going to blow up the moon. We have to get out of here!" He held up the detonator. *Four minutes.*

"Is it enough time?"

Harry bit his lip. "Let's find out."

Ava shuffled back to let Harry settle himself at the handlebars. He straddled the bike and tapped at the Stallion's control panel, routing all non-essential power to the Stallion's thrusters. "Here we go ..." he muttered.

With a twist of the throttle they were away and banking steeply.

Harry crouched low, and Ava clung on tight behind him. The bike shuddered beneath them as he pushed it further, harder than he ever had before. Soon it was shaking as though it might fall apart, rivets and all.

He cast a glance behind and saw the desert receding. He saw Vellis's base, the refinery, the cobweb of trenches that Kerbrus had dug. The droid itself lay sprawled on the sands.

Three minutes.

He tried to calculate their speed and the distance. Could they make it?

"Come in, Harry." Harkman's voice, crackling over the comms.

"I read you."

"We've got them. We've got Tim and Alanna." This time Zo's voice was choked with joy. "I don't know what happened down there but—"

"Leave!" barked Harry. "Get out of there! The moon's going to blow."

A brief silence, while the Stallion streaked higher and higher from Gwildor's surface.

"We can't," said Harkman, at last. "Not without you."

"You can, and you will," shouted Harry.

His eyes were blurry with tears. "This can't have all been for nothing."

"Mum," said Ava. "If you stay, we'll all die. Please … don't be foolish."

Looking ahead, Harry could see the distant glint of the Tagus, hanging in orbit above them.

It seemed a very long way off.

Another silence on the line. Then Achebe's voice. Harry had never heard it so broken before.

"I love you."

"I love you too, Mum," said Ava, thickly.

Then, nothing.

"They understand," said Harry. "They must do."

One minute.

"Ain't got much left in the tank, partner," said the Stallion's robotic voice.

Harry looked back again. He could see all of the moon now, hanging in space. They were away. *But not far enough.* Up ahead, the Tagus was getting smaller.

We're alone.

He took one hand from the bars to check the detonator.

00:03 …

00:02 …

00:01 …

There was no sound, apart from Ava's soft gasp, over the comms. Harry's heart was in his mouth.

It was strangely beautiful. A blue

explosion, unimaginably vast. It bloomed like the petals of a flower, then began to die, shrivelling at the edges. At the same time, its centre turned black, like an expanding pupil in a giant blue eye.

The Stallion juddered and slowed, as though they were riding through treacle. The screens flickered, and the Space Stallion's voice came fainter than ever.

"Till next time, partner."

Over his shoulder, Harry saw Gwildor had vanished. A whole moon – gone.

And in its place was pure blackness, a yawning cosmic well with no bottom, tugging them backwards.

At least Vellis's weapon was gone too.

They were moving in reverse now,

slowly at first, then faster. They were sinking. Drowning. And there was no way back.

"I think … I think Vellis was right," said Harry, heavily. "I think it's over."

"Don't say that," muttered Ava. Harry couldn't see her, but he could tell she was trying not to cry. He couldn't blame her.

"I'm sorry," he said. "This is all my fault."

"Don't say that either," snorted Ava. "You're a great cadet, Harry." She hesitated. "You're a great friend."

"You too, Ava."

"How's about me, partner?"

Harry gasped. Looking down, he

saw that the main control screen had flickered into life one last time. He twisted the throttle.

One last burst from the thrusters. For a moment they were caught in a battle of forces, gravity from the black hole fighting against the forward propulsion from the engines. They hung in the balance, until, millimetre by millimetre, they crept forwards.

"We're doing it!" yelled Harry.

They picked up speed, every second tearing them further free from the invisible pull of the Tallium detonation.

"What *happened*?" stammered Ava.

"Backup power," croaked Harry, patting the Stallion's flank. "Like Zo always says. Got to have a little backup handy."

All the way back to Vantia1, Harry sat strapped in between his parents at the rear of the Tagus. They didn't speak. There would be plenty of time for that later. But they held him tightly, as though they would never let him go.

And I won't let you go either, Mum and Dad. Never again.

Harry had a strange feeling inside him. A calmness he couldn't remember experiencing before. Like he'd finally reached a destination that had seemed too far away.

His mum rested her head on his, and his dad smiled at him, his eyes glistening.

Harry smiled back.

Over his dad's shoulder, he could see Ava clinging to her own mother. Admiral Achebe had given up her seat in the cockpit to be closer to her. Harry's trusty old Space Stallion rested up against a console, no longer hidden from view. Ahead of it sat Zo, talking to the navigator, grinning and laughing more than Harry had seen in years.

Everyone he loved was here. All together at last.

Beyond, through the viewing screen, was the endless blackness of space.

As he stared into it, Harry found his features creasing into a frown.

There was terrible danger out there, still. They had escaped. But so, he suspected, had their enemy. Harkman had ordered scans to try and trace Vellis's direction of travel, but they'd come back empty. "He might not have made it out," Achebe had said.

But no one really believed that.

Somehow, Harry had a feeling that this wasn't the end.

I'll find you, Vellis, he promised himself. *Wherever you go, wherever you are ... I'm coming for you.*

The End